READ with me!

Magic music

by WILLIAM MURRAY
stories by JILL CORBY
illustrated by STUART TROTTER

Ladybird Books

Tom and Kate are at home. They can't go outside.

"I like to play with this boat," says Tom. "It can go over here and under there."

"Come and look at this book," Kate tells him. "It has lots of animals in it. That's a giraffe and this is a crocodile," she says. "And there's a baby one."

READ with me! *has been written using about 800 words and these include the 300 Key Words.*

In the first six books, all words introduced occur again in the following book to provide vital repetition in the early stages. The number of new words increases as the child gains confidence and progresses through the stories.

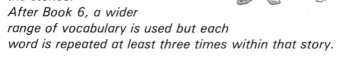

After Book 6, a wider range of vocabulary is used but each word is repeated at least three times within that story.

The stories centre on the everyday lives of Kate, Tom, Sam the dog, Mum, Dad, friends, neighbours and relations. This setting often provides a springboard into Tom and Kate's world of make-believe. Also, the humorous, colourful illustrations include picture story sequences to stimulate the reader's own language and imagination.

A complete list of stories is given on the back cover and suggestions for using each book are made on the back pages.

Further details about this reading scheme plus a card listing the 300 Key Words are contained in the Parent/ Teacher Guide.

This book belongs to

_____

_____

British Library Cataloguing in Publication Data
Murray, W. (William), *(date)*
    Magic music.
    1. English language—Readers
    I. Title   II. Corby, Jill   III. Trotter, Stuart   IV. Series
    428.6
    ISBN 0-7214-1323-4

First edition

Published by Ladybird Books Ltd Loughborough Leicestershire UK
Ladybird Books Inc Auburn Maine 04210 USA

Printed in England (3)

Their mother tells them that Uncle Matt will be coming today. He is from Australia and has come all the way from Australia to see them.

Tom and Kate want to see what he looks like. Dad tells them that they must get ready for Uncle Matt.

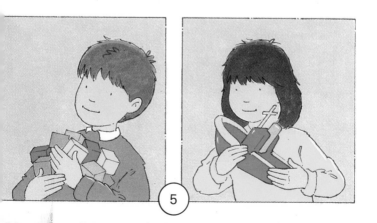

Tom and Kate see Uncle Matt's car coming.

What has he got? Two big boxes and two little ones. These came from Australia. What is in the boxes? Tom and Kate can't wait to see.

"You look very well," Mother tells him.

"And so do you," Uncle Matt says.
"You all look very well." He talks
about Australia. Then he says,
"These two big ones are for you two.
This is for you, Kate. And Tom, this
one is yours. The two little ones are
for your mum and dad," says Uncle
Matt. "You can see what's in your
boxes now, if you like."

Tom and Kate look at their boxes.
What can be in them?

Tom looks into his box. He sees lots of things that make music. He takes out the cymbals.

"Listen Kate, just listen to this," he tells her.

8

Kate looks into her big box. She sees lots of zoo animals. She takes out the elephant.

"Look at this elephant," she tells Tom. "And under here, there's a baby penguin."

They have lots of things in their boxes and they take everything out. Tom can make music now and Kate can play with all her zoo animals. They are very pleased with all the things Uncle Matt got for them in Australia.

"Kate and Tom, are you ready?" asks their mother. "We must eat now," she tells them.

"Uncle Matt will be ready to eat by now," Father says. "Come over here and sit down, everyone."

"Here is your drink, Kate. And Tom, this is your drink," says Father. "What can I get for you to drink, Uncle Matt?" Father asks.

Uncle Matt talks some more about Australia.

"Will you have some of this, Uncle Matt?" asks Mother. "Kate, give this to him please," Mother tells her.

"And Tom, here is yours," says his dad.

"Have we all got everything?" asks Dad. "Then we can all eat."

Then they all sit down and talk. Kate
plays with her zoo animals. She
makes the giraffes run races. Then
she takes away the one that wins,
and they have some more races.

Some have fallen down, so they can't
win. She is very pleased with her zoo
animals.

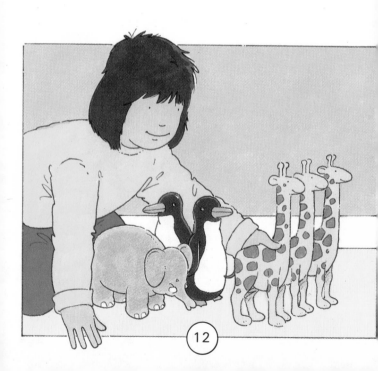

Tom makes music with his cymbals.
He is very pleased with all his music
things as well.

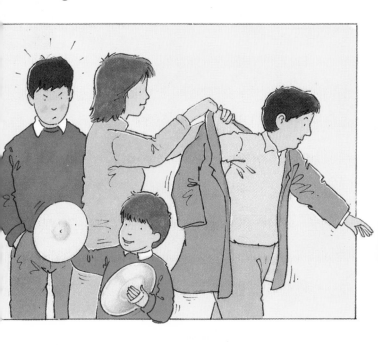

Uncle Matt likes to see them play
with the toys. But now he has to go
and see some other boys and girls.
They all go with him to the car. Then
away he goes.

Then Kate sees Tom's trumpet. She takes it and plays it.

"Listen to me," she says.

"That's mine," Tom shouts. "Give it to me."

"No," she says, "I want a turn now."

Tom wants his trumpet but Kate will not give it to him.

So Tom takes her giraffe and makes it go round and round, up high.

"That's mine," shouts Kate. "You can't have it."

But Tom will not give her the giraffe.

15

Kate is not pleased, so she takes Tom's drum.

"Put that drum down, it's mine," he shouts.

"It's mine now," Kate tells him. "I've got it now."

Tom takes her crocodile and puts it up high.

"No," she shouts at him. "Give me my crocodile. It's mine."

Father does not like the way they shout. He is not pleased with them at all.

"Just look at what you have done," he says.

"Put everything away now, then you two can go to bed," he tells them.

Tom and Kate are very sad. They get into their beds.

Tom has his music things by his bed and Kate has her zoo animals by her bed. They are very sad that they can't play now. Kate looks at her things and Tom looks at his things.

"It was good to see Uncle Matt,"
says Dad, "and very good of him to
get the things for Kate and Tom."

"But Tom wasn't good, and Kate
wasn't good," Mum says. "I must
talk to them about it."

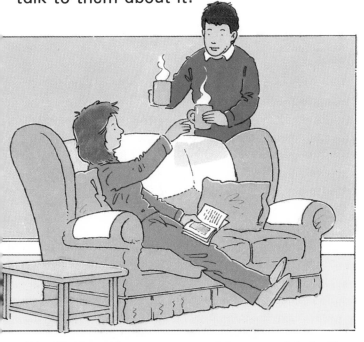

"I shall make us something to drink,"
says Dad. "Here is your drink, and
this is mine."

"Look at all the penguins coming in. There are lots of them all over my bed now. They are everywhere," says Tom.

The penguins are jumping up and down all over Tom's bed. If he stops playing the triangle the penguins stop. The music makes them hop and jump.

"If I want them to keep on jumping, I have to play the triangle," Tom says.

Tom goes to
get Kate.

"Kate, Kate,
listen, Kate.
You must get up
and come with
me," he tells her.
"Look at this, Kate," he says.

"You have got my penguins. You
can't have them," she tells him.
"Look, one has fallen over."

"No, Kate, it wasn't like that," he says. "I will tell you about it. They just came. They all came in. They came for the music. Look, if I play this way, they hop and jump all over my bed. If I stop, they all stop. Just look," he tells her.

"Can I have a go, please, Tom?" she asks.

He gives her the triangle and she plays for the penguins. They all jump about, on and off the bed.

"What will come if I play this drum?"
Kate asks Tom.

She plays the drum and lots of
elephants come in. She stops the
music and the elephants stop. She
plays some more and they go up onto
the bed.

Tom plays the triangle and the penguins
hop and jump round the elephants.

"This is good," Kate tells Tom.
"What shall we play now?"

Tom looks at his music things.

"What do you want to play, Kate?" he asks her.

"Can I have a go with your tambourine, please?" she says.

He gives her the tambourine.

"What shall I play?" he asks her.

"Have a go with the cymbals," she tells him.

As Kate plays the tambourine, lots of crocodiles come in.

"Look, Tom," she says, "all these crocodiles are coming in."

Tom plays the cymbals.

"What will come in now?" he asks.

Lots of kangaroos come in, hop, hop, hop.

"Look at the baby kangaroo," says Kate.

Tom says, "Kangaroos come from Australia. Will the crocodiles want to eat the others?" asks Tom. "We can't play if the crocodiles want to eat all the others."

"We shall just have to see what the crocodiles do," Kate tells him. And just as before, if Tom stops the music, the crocodiles stop.

"They don't look as if they want to eat the other animals at all," Tom says.

"What animal will come if I play the recorder?" Kate asks Tom. "Will it be the lions?"

"Will it be the giraffes?" Tom asks. "Play the recorder, Kate, and see what comes in."

She plays the recorder and lots of giraffes come running in.

"They can't eat us," she tells Tom, "and they don't eat the others. That's good."

"There is just one more thing to play," Tom tells Kate.

He takes up the trumpet and plays it. Lots of lions run in. "Stop, stop," says Kate. "The lions will eat the others. Lions like to eat everything."

"I shall stop if the lions want to eat the others," Tom tells her.

"I shall see if I can play two things," Tom says.

He takes the recorder and the cymbals, and plays them. Now he can't stop to say something. If he stops, the animals will stop as well.

"You have got the kangaroos jumping and the giraffes running everywhere," Kate tells him. "And look at this one."

"I shall have a go with two things now," she says. "What shall I have? The drum and the trumpet. I can do it this way."

She plays the drum and the trumpet. The elephants go first, then the lions go running round. The lions run faster than the elephants.

"Can we play all the things and make all the animals go?" Tom asks Kate.

"We shall see," Kate tells him. "I shall take these."

She puts on
the drum.
She takes the
tambourine
and the trumpet
and plays them.
It works!
She can make
music with
all the things.

She goes round and round, and the lions, the elephants and the crocodiles all go with her. She goes up over the bed and the animals go up over the bed as well. They go round and round. Then Kate stops and looks at Tom.

Tom takes the other music things. He takes the recorder, the triangle and the cymbals. He can just play them all.

The other animals come to him. They like the music. The giraffes come running, the kangaroos are jumping about and the penguins hop up to him.

Now Tom goes round and all the
animals go round with him. They go
up over the bed, round and round,
then down under the bed. They are
everywhere.

"We shall play everything," Tom says to Kate. "We can see if all the animals will come with us."

So they play all the music things.

"Kate, look at my dragon," Tom says. "The dragon is coming as well."

"It's strange to see the dragon coming with us," Kate says.

Down they all go, off the bed. Up over this and down off that. Round here and under there. The animals are everywhere.

The dragon likes the music and Tom and Kate like to see it coming with them.

"I do like this, Kate," says Tom.

"And so do I," she tells him. "It's fun."

"Are Mum and Dad in bed?" Kate asks Tom.

"We shall have to go and see," Tom tells her.

They put down all the music things and all the animals stay where they are.

They go to see their mum and dad.

"Yes," says Tom. "They are in bed. They don't know that we are not in bed."

"That's a good thing," Kate tells him. "We must put all the things away now. Wasn't it fun?"

Tom puts all the music things away.
Then he helps Kate put the dragon
and the other animals away. They
look everywhere for them. One
penguin has fallen down. Tom puts it
away. Then they get into their beds.

"Tom and Kate, get up now please," says Mum.

"Come on, you two, come and eat," she tells them.

"Some of this, Kate?" her mum asks. "What do you want to eat, Tom?"

"Now we can play with our things that Uncle Matt got from Australia for us," Tom tells Kate. "I shall play with them here."

"So shall I," Kate says. "We can have fun today. Tom can play with my animals," Kate tells her mum and dad.

"And Kate can play with my music things," Tom tells them.

"We can play very well now," they say.

Words introduced in this book

Number of words used............................26

Look at the pictures and read the words.
Which word is missing?

Kate plays Tom's

..t.rump.et............

(trumpet, tambourine, drum)

Tom plays the

...cymbals............

(cymbals, recorder,
trumpet)

The ...elephant....
comes in.
(lion, elephant,
kangaroo)

Tom has Kate's ...crocodile
(crocodile, penguin)

Notes for using this book

The words, pictures and planning of this book are designed to:

* help the child to learn to read
* help you to make learning an exciting and enjoyable experience for her*
* encourage lots of conversation
* help her to become confident in her own ability
* encourage her powers of observation, understanding and sense of humour.

When your child is ready and keen to learn to read (a Reading Readiness checklist is given in the Parent/Teacher Guide) *introduce this book just like any other picture storybook. Find a quiet, comfortable place and either read the book all the way through or read and talk about one page at a time. Point to the words and show that reading goes from left to right.*